Princess Power

To Ms. Wilson's royal readers —

❧ The Awfully Angry Ogre ❧

See with your hearts!

By Suzanne Williams
Illustrated by Chuck Gonzales

HarperCollins*Publishers*

Suzanne Williams

2007

Library of Congress Cataloging-in-Publication Data
Williams, Suzanne, 1949–
  The awfully angry ogre / by Suzanne Willams ; illustrated by Chuck
Gonzales. — 1st Harper Trophy ed.
      p.   cm.—(Princess Power ; #3)
  Summary: During the princesses' visit to nine-year-old Princess Tansy's
home, they must confront an angry ogre on Mount Majesta to save her
brothers from being turned to stone.
  ISBN-10: 0-06-078303-6 — ISBN-13: 978-0-06-078303-7
  ISBN-10: 0-06-078302-8 (pbk.) — ISBN-13: 978-0-06-078302-0 (pbk.)
  [1. Princesses—Fiction. 2. Friendship—Fiction. 3. Magic—Fiction.
4. Brothers—Fiction. 5. Adventure and adventurers—Fiction.] I.Gonzales,
Chuck, ill. II.Title.
PZ7.W66824Aw 2007   2006017884
[E]—dc22   CIP
                                                                   AC

Typography by Jennifer Heuer
1 2 3 4 5 6 7 8 9 10

First Edition

To Rosemary Brosnan and
Rachel Orr, with heartfelt thanks

Contents

Princess Tansy

PRINCESS TANSY WOKE WITH A START. SOMEONE was knocking on her door. "Just a minute!" she called out, pushing back the bedcovers. Tansy shivered in the chilly morning air that seeped through the cracks in her family's castle. Grabbing her faded robe, she wrapped it around herself tightly, then hopped across the cold stone floor to open the door.

Tansy's room was at the top of a tower.

She'd recently chosen the room to get away from her six brothers. Before she moved, they'd made her life miserable, teasing her and playing practical jokes, such as putting frogs and snakes in her bed. Fortunately, none of them liked climbing the narrow, winding staircase to her room and only came up to fetch her for a meal or to deliver a message. Edward, her oldest brother and worst tormentor, refused to come up for any reason. That suited Tansy just fine.

Tansy scraped her door open. "Good morning, lazybones," said her brother Jonah. At fourteen, Jonah was five years older than Tansy. Even though he could be just as mischievous as the others, he was Tansy's favorite. Jonah painted the most beautiful pictures— especially of Mount Majesta, which towered over the family castle. A dozen of Jonah's paintings hung in Tansy's room.

Rubbing the sleep from her eyes, Tansy said, "What are you talking about? It's early!"

Jonah grinned. Like Tansy, he was slim and freckled, with ginger-colored hair. Only he was about ten inches taller than Tansy, who hadn't yet reached five feet. "Early for you, maybe," said Jonah. "I've been up since dawn." Jonah often rose early. Sunrise was his favorite time to paint Mount Majesta.

"So, what's up?" Tansy stifled a yawn.

"Besides you and me?" asked Jonah. "No one else in this family, that's for sure. They're all still snoring away."

Tansy frowned. "Then why did you get me up?"

"Maybe I just wanted some company," Jonah said with a smile. He paused as if remembering something. "Oh yeah. And someone's trying to reach you through the crystal ball."

"Why didn't you say so right away?" Tansy pushed past him and started down the steps to the Crystal Ball Room. "Did you see who it was?" she called back over her shoulder.

"Some girl with wavy blond hair."

Princess Lysandra! Tansy hadn't seen her friend in a couple of months, though they'd chatted a few times. The last time they'd been together—along with the princesses Fatima and Elena—they'd stayed with Fatima's sister and brother-in-law in their fabulous marble palace. She could still picture the rich silk tapestries lining every wall, and the gorgeous lake and gardens. The visit had turned out to be quite an adventure.

Tansy wound down the steps to the ground floor, then raced to the Crystal Ball Room and squeezed inside. No bigger than a wardrobe, the room was mirrored on three sides to make it seem larger, and a fake fireplace had been painted on the fourth wall. Tissue flowers, vaguely resembling roses, sat in a vase on top of a fake marble-topped table. Anyone looking in on her family through the crystal ball would see this room, so her family tried to make it look nice. Still, Tansy doubted their efforts hid how poor they really were.

Lysandra's image floated in the ball. She was bent over a piece of paper, writing. Tansy had visited Lysandra's palace, so she knew nothing was fake about *her* family's grand Crystal Ball Room.

Lysandra glanced up. "Oh, hi," she said "I didn't think you were in, so I was going to leave you a note."

"My brother Jonah saw you. He came and told me."

Lysandra's face moved closer to the ball. She squinted at Tansy. "You're in your robe, aren't you? Did I get you out of bed? I forgot about the time difference. It's two hours earlier where you live, isn't it?"

"That's okay," said Tansy. She hoped Lysandra couldn't tell how faded her robe was. She didn't like to ask her parents for a new one with the royal treasury at an all-time

low. "What's up?"

"I'm bored out of my skull," Lysandra said with a sigh. "Things are so dull around here that I almost wish Gabriella hadn't gotten married and moved away. Even listening to her nag was something to do."

Tansy laughed. Gabriella was Lysandra's older sister. If given the choice, Tansy would take one nagging sister over six annoying brothers any day, but she didn't say so. Instead, she said, "We need to get together again soon."

Lysandra's face brightened. "Exactly what I was thinking. In fact, I already talked to Elena and Fatima, and we'd like to come visit you, if that's all right. We could even be there in a few days. Fatima's offered to fly all three of us on her carpet."

"Fantastic!" Tansy exclaimed, panicking at the same time. Her family's small castle was an embarrassment compared with the grand castles and palaces of the other princesses. What would the girls think of the way Tansy lived? Still, she couldn't very well tell them *not* to come. That would be rude! Besides, she really wanted to see her friends. Tansy bit her lip. "I'd love for you to visit."

"Great," said Lysandra. "I'll contact the others. See you soon!"

As she sat in the Crystal Ball Room, Tansy hoped having everyone come wouldn't turn out to be a mistake.

The Ogre

WHEN HER PARENTS CAME DOWNSTAIRS FOR breakfast, Tansy joined them at the long oak table. "My friends want to visit in a few days," she said. "I told them it was okay, but if you don't think this is a good time, that's fine." Tansy paused, half hoping her parents would say they couldn't possibly host anyone right now. Then she could suggest that the princesses meet somewhere else. Maybe they could all go to Elena's home instead. They'd never been there either.

But Queen Charlotte, a cheerful, plump woman with dimpled cheeks, just smiled. "I think that sounds like a lovely idea," she said, pouring herself a cup of tea. "Your father and I would enjoy meeting your friends, wouldn't we, dear?"

King Albert glanced up from his copy of *The Majesta Daily*. Though his long, crooked nose and dark, shaggy eyebrows gave him a rather stern appearance, he was quite reasonable most of the time. "Sure. Why not? The more the merrier, I suppose." He turned back to his paper.

Well, that's that, thought Tansy. She hoped her friends wouldn't be *too* disappointed when they saw what her house was like.

Shouts and heavy boots sounded on the stairs, and Tansy's brothers Edward and James clomped into the room. "Scoot over, squirt," growled Edward. He jabbed her with his elbow as he plopped onto the bench beside her.

"Watch it!" Tansy jabbed him back.

Edward only laughed and reached across the table to grab a platter of sausages. At nineteen, he was strong and muscular, with the same dark, shaggy eyebrows as King Albert but a much straighter nose. Edward was very interested in girls, and it puzzled Tansy that they seemed to like him, too. She found him hotheaded and rude.

James sat down heavily on Tansy's other side, squishing her between himself and Edward. Short and compact, with their mother's sandy hair and freckles, James was two years younger than Edward. When Edward wasn't around to influence him, he could be good-natured. But if Edward was present, James followed his lead.

James grabbed a large plum from the fruit bowl, stuffed the whole thing in his mouth, and started chewing. Juice spurted from the corners of his mouth and ran down his chin.

"Really, James!" scolded Queen Charlotte. "Your table manners are atrocious!"

"Sorry, Mother," James apologized. But as soon as she looked away, he grinned at Edward.

Tansy glared at them. *They*—along with her other four brothers—might turn out to be a worse embarrassment than the castle!

"Anything interesting in the news today, dear?" Queen Charlotte asked, sipping her tea.

King Albert frowned. "There was a fire in the Three Foxes Tavern last night. And two sheep have gone missing from one of the villagers' fields."

Edward stabbed at the air with his fork. "The ogre set that fire! And he's responsible for the missing sheep, too. Everybody says so."

"That's right," James mumbled through a mouthful of food.

King Albert raised an eyebrow. "Just because everybody says something doesn't make it true. There are other explanations for fires and missing sheep."

Queen Charlotte nodded. "Careless

mistakes and wolves, for example." She rose from her chair. "Please excuse me," she said. "I need to wake the other boys."

Tansy stayed at the table, listening eagerly. The ogre was camped halfway up Mount Majesta. He had first appeared in the kingdom eight years ago, when Tansy was only a baby.

"Someone *saw* the ogre set the fire," Edward insisted. "Said he came down in the middle of the night and hurled a burning log through a window."

"People see all sorts of things when they want to," King Albert replied. "Did anyone find the ogre's footprints near the tavern?"

Edward wiped his hand across his mouth. "Don't know. I didn't hear anything about that."

"Maybe he erased them," said James.

The King snorted. "Rumors," he said. "All

rumors. Anything bad that happens, people blame it on the ogre—even failed crops and plagues. Yet there's not a shred of proof he's ventured into town even once."

"Still," Edward said, "the kingdom would be a lot better off with the ogre gone."

Edward was right, thought Tansy. No matter *what* the ogre had or hadn't done, people were frightened of him. And because of that, many townsfolk—including several of her family's former servants—had moved away to other kingdoms. With fewer and fewer people to work and pay taxes, the kingdom had become poorer and poorer.

"So how would *you* get the ogre to leave?" King Albert asked with a sigh.

Tansy thought that was a good question. Anyone who had ever tried to approach the ogre was turned into stone. This had happened to some hotheaded young man every year for the past eight years. Eight granite statues now circled the well in the meadow where the ogre lived.

Edward stroked his straggly beard. "I'm not sure, but James and I will find a way to drive him off." He made a tight fist. "And if the ogre refuses to go, we'll kill him."

James grinned at his brother. "Yeah."

King Albert shook his head. "And what makes you think *you* wouldn't end up as blocks of granite too?"

"We're stronger and smarter than those other men," said Edward, flexing his muscles. "Right, James?"

"Right. And if we don't succeed, you can always use us to mend the castle walls."

"Not funny," King Albert said. "You're talking foolishness. Leave the ogre alone, and he'll leave *us* alone."

"You don't know that," argued Edward. "Even if the ogre *didn't* do any of those things he's been accused of, he could still strike at any time!"

"I absolutely forbid the two of you to go anywhere near that ogre," King Albert said firmly. "Understand?"

Nodding sullenly, Edward stood to leave. James scrambled up from the bench to go with him. Before he left, Edward thumped Tansy on the back of the head. "Ow!" she said, though he hadn't really done it very hard. "Cut that out!"

The king frowned at Edward. "Sorry," he apologized. "I don't know what came over me." Whistling, he sauntered off, with James right behind him. Tansy glared at Edward, thinking again how glad she was that he couldn't be bothered to climb to her tower room.

As usual, her brothers had left without cleaning up after themselves. With a sigh, Tansy began stacking the dishes. The kitchen maid who used to clear the table had moved away only a few days ago. Apparently the maid's parents were convinced the ogre had caused their cow to stop producing milk.

"If you ask me," Tansy said to her father, "Edward and James only want to go after the ogre to impress girls."

King Albert gave her a small smile. "I hadn't thought of that, but you could be right."

Tansy carried the dirty dishes into the kitchen. She agreed with her father that it was foolish to go looking for trouble. But she also understood her brothers' excitement at the idea of fighting an ogre.

As Tansy washed the dishes, she thought

about how Lysandra and her other friends would arrive in a few days. If she'd told them about the ogre, would they still have wanted to come? Probably, she decided. In fact, she could just imagine Lysandra saying, "An ogre? Wonderful! I've never seen an ogre before!" The thought made Tansy grin.

The Princesses Arrive

THREE DAYS LATER TANSY WATCHED FROM HER tower bedroom for the princesses' arrival. When she spotted a flying carpet skimming over the trees, she raced outside to greet her friends.

Fatima landed the carpet on the grassy lawn in front of the castle, and the princesses all hopped off. After they'd hugged one another and exclaimed over how excited they were to be together again, Fatima rolled up her carpet and strapped it onto her back. She was beautiful, with dark skin and long black hair. At twelve, Fatima was also the oldest of the four girls.

"What a fantastic flight," Fatima said, brushing a speck of dirt from her pink blouse and smoothing down her purple pantaloons. "It was clear and sunny the whole way."

Lysandra looped her wavy blond hair behind her ears. She was ten, just a year older than Tansy. "We could see everything down below. We even saw whales spouting when we flew over the ocean. It was wonderful!"

"And we passed by the most beautiful birds," eleven-year-old Elena added.

"Sounds great," said Tansy, as she led her friends up to the castle's front doors.

She hoped the flight wouldn't turn out to be the best part of their trip; her friends were bound to be disappointed by the drabness of her family's castle. Tansy crossed her fingers that they wouldn't be too uncomfortable there. And then there was the matter of her brothers. She could only pray they'd be on their best behavior while her guests were visiting.

But no sooner had the girls entered the Main Hall than Cole and Ethan, Tansy's two

younger brothers, sprang out from behind a large potted fern.

"Boo!" they shouted, making the princesses jump.

"Bats and bullfrogs!" Fatima exclaimed.

Cole grinned. "Scared you, didn't we?" He was seven, and Ethan was eight, but the two of them looked so much alike with their red hair

and blue eyes that they could've passed for twins. Laughing, the boys ran off without even waiting to be introduced.

Tansy rolled her eyes. "Those were Cole and Ethan," she said. "I'm sorry to say they're my brothers. I did warn you that I have *six*, didn't I?"

Elena smiled. "You did."

Tansy's parents rose from the couch when the princesses entered the Sitting Room. Raising his shaggy eyebrows, King Albert declared, "These must be the young ladies we've heard so much about."

"Please make yourselves at home," Queen Charlotte said cheerfully. "We're so pleased to meet you at last."

After some pleasant conversation, the girls bid Tansy's parents farewell. As they climbed the narrow, winding staircase to Tansy's room,

Fatima said, "I like your parents. They seem very nice." Tansy noticed her friend didn't say anything about Cole and Ethan.

"Wow, your room is really high!" Lysandra exclaimed halfway up the stairs. Elena didn't say a word, but Tansy could hear her huffing and puffing behind them.

"Sorry about the climb," apologized Tansy. "I wanted to be as far away from my brothers as I could get."

At last they arrived at her room. Lysandra kicked off her shoes and sank onto Tansy's bed. Stretching out her legs, she exclaimed, "Ah! That feels *so* good!"

Elena walked around the room, examining every painting. "We flew over that mountain," she said. "What's it called?"

"Mount Majesta," said Tansy.

"Did you paint these?" asked Elena.

"They're very good."

With pride, Tansy said, "My brother Jonah painted them. As brothers go, he's not so bad. Better than the rest, anyway."

"What a fabulous view!" Fatima exclaimed suddenly, staring out the window.

Tansy went to stand beside her. In the distance Mount Majesta rose tall and regal, clothed in a forest-green cloak and wearing a hat of snow. "It *is* beautiful, isn't it?" she said. She felt glad that at least the view from the castle was grand. Perhaps to impress Fatima even more, she added, "You know, there's an ogre living halfway up the mountain."

Fatima's mouth dropped open. "You're kidding!"

"Really?" Lysandra and Elena exclaimed.

Tansy grinned. "It's true." She plopped onto her bed next to Lysandra and invited the others to do the same. It was a good thing her bed was wide since they'd all have to sleep together during the visit!

Tansy told her friends everything she knew about the ogre, including the rumors that he stole sheep and set fires. She'd just finished telling them about the eight young men who'd been turned into stone when there was a loud knock at her door.

The princesses jumped, then laughed at themselves for being so startled. Tansy hopped off her bed and scraped open the door.

Jonah stood in the doorway, panting and holding the handles of several large bags. "These just arrived," he said, dumping them inside the room. He glanced over at Tansy's friends. "I guess none of you believes in traveling light, do you?" But he was smiling as he said it.

Tansy introduced Jonah to everyone.

"Thanks for lugging our things upstairs," Fatima said. "I had to send them by carriage. They never would've fit on my carpet."

"Plus, our bags are so heavy, she probably couldn't have gotten the carpet off the ground," added Lysandra.

Tansy patted her brother's arm. "Good thing you're so strong."

Jonah tried to flex but only managed a small bump. "Not at all like Edward's," he said sadly.

"Who cares?" said Tansy. "Edward may have bigger muscles, but you've got a bigger *brain*."

"You're right, of course," Jonah said with a grin.

"I love your paintings," Elena said softly.

Jonah blushed to the roots of his ginger hair. "Thanks." He started to leave, then turned back again. "Forgot to tell you. Mom said dinner will be ready in about ten minutes."

At dinner the princesses met Tansy's other brothers: Edward, James, and twelve-year-old Matthew. To Tansy's relief, Edward and James made an effort to have better table manners, eating more slowly than usual and asking for things instead of lunging across the table.

Elena and Jonah, who were sitting across from each other, got into a discussion about poetry and art. At the other end of the table, James chattered away with Fatima. Even shy Matthew, seated beside Lysandra, became quite talkative during the meal.

After dinner King Albert and Queen Charlotte excused themselves to talk with a group of villagers who were upset about the latest ogre rumors. Tansy's brothers left too— except for Jonah and Matthew, who stayed to clear the dishes from the table. The other princesses must have been surprised that there weren't any servants to do the job, but they jumped up to help too. Tansy's face went warm. "We can do this by ourselves. You can go relax."

"Nonsense," said Fatima. "It'll be fun."

"Matthew and I can stack and carry the plates," said Lysandra.

"And I'll help Jonah with the drinking glasses," added Elena.

Tansy filled the sink with soap and water, and they all took turns scrubbing and rinsing the dishes. They slopped most of the water on themselves but had a great time.

Later that night, the princesses wearily climbed the stairs to Tansy's room to get ready for bed. Lysandra brushed her wavy blond hair. "Your brothers are much nicer than I thought they'd be," she told Tansy. "I think Matthew's really sweet."

Elena pulled her nightgown over her head. "Jonah's going to let me watch him paint sometime."

Tansy grinned. "I hope you like getting up

early, then." She was sitting cross-legged on her bed, polishing her wooden flute with a rag. The flute was magical, and Tansy carried it with her everywhere. Whenever she played it, the thoughts of anyone near could be heard as if spoken aloud. Her flute often helped her uncover the mischief her brothers were up to. But so far their behavior had been better than she'd expected. Even Cole and Ethan hadn't been too awful, in spite of the scare they'd given the girls earlier that day.

Tansy was also glad that her friends didn't seem to care that the castle was in bad shape. They'd even thought clearing the table and doing the dishes was *fun*!

Fatima kicked off her sandals and hopped onto Tansy's bed. "James said he and Edward are going on a hunting trip tomorrow."

"Oh?" said Tansy. She wasn't very surprised. Her two oldest brothers often hunted for deer and rabbit.

"He said they might be gone a couple of days. Then he added something else kind of odd." She paused, as if remembering. "He said, 'This time we'll be hunting for *really* big game.'"

Tansy stopped polishing her flute, suddenly alert. "Did he say what he meant by that?"

Fatima shrugged. "I asked him if he meant elephants, but I was joking, of course. I know there aren't any elephants around here. Anyway, James just smiled and said, 'Much bigger game than that.' You don't suppose he was talking about that ogre, do you?"

Tansy hugged herself worriedly. It was *exactly* what she thought.

Gone Hunting

"YOUR BROTHERS WOULDN'T REALLY GO AFTER an ogre, would they?" asked Elena. Her hazel eyes shone with concern.

Tansy bit her lip. "They want to go after it. But my father forbids them."

"You don't think they'd go anyway, do you?" Fatima asked.

"I don't know," said Tansy. "I hope not, but who can tell with those two?"

"I bet James was just talking big," said Lysandra. "Boys do that, you know."

Lysandra was probably right, thought Tansy. But even so, she found it hard not to worry.

The next morning, when the girls went downstairs for breakfast, Queen Charlotte and Matthew were already eating. Matthew blushed when Lysandra sat down beside him.

"Have Edward and James left to go hunting yet?" Tansy asked.

Her mother nodded. "They left before your father and I were up," she said, passing around a basket of apple tarts. "They promised last night they'd bring back some rabbits for dinner."

The princesses exchanged worried looks. James had said they might be gone a couple of days. And rabbits certainly weren't "big game."

"When did they leave?" Tansy asked.

"I'm not sure," her mother replied. "But Jonah might know."

After the girls finished breakfast, they went outside to search for Jonah. Matthew came too. Walking alongside Lysandra, he told her the names of all the trees and wildflowers growing near the castle. He loved studying nature.

They found Jonah in the field behind the

castle, finishing a painting of Mount Majesta. As usual, he'd been up with the sun.

"How did you make the snow on the mountain look so real?" Elena asked, admiring the picture. "I can almost *feel* how cold it is."

Jonah beamed, obviously pleased at Elena's interest. He started to launch into an explanation of his painting techniques, but Tansy interrupted. "Did you see Edward and James

go off this morning?"

"Sure did." He rubbed his freckled nose, leaving a smudge of blue paint. "They left about two hours ago. Their poor horses were loaded down with so much stuff, it looked like they were going off to war!"

This news alarmed Tansy and her friends. Excusing themselves, they started back to the castle.

"I imagine we're all thinking the same thing," said Elena.

Tansy nodded. "We've got to stop them! If we took your flying carpet, could we catch up to them, Fatima?"

"Of course," she said.

"Then let's go!" said Lysandra.

Soon the four princesses were sailing over the forest toward Mount Majesta. Tansy had thought it would be easy to spot Edward and James from the air, but the trees were so thick and leafy, it was impossible to see the ground.

"Where does the ogre live?" Lysandra asked.

Tansy pointed north, toward a clearing about halfway up the mountain, and Fatima steered the carpet in that direction. When they neared the ogre's camp, the princesses saw a stone well in a meadow. Tansy counted eight granite statues surrounding the well. She

sighed with relief. At least there weren't any *new* ones.

The ogre was nowhere in sight.

"Where now?" Fatima asked after they'd circled the meadow a couple of times.

"I don't know," Tansy admitted.

The princesses finally landed at the edge of a small lake. Tucked between the trees, but

close to the shore, stood a trim white cottage.

"Let's ask whoever lives there if they've seen my brothers," Tansy said.

Fatima rolled up her carpet and strapped it onto her back. As the princesses approached the cottage, they heard someone singing in a dry, raspy voice. It sounded like a key rattling in a rusty lock. When they knocked on the door, the singing stopped. Then the door creaked open, and a wrinkled and bony old woman stared out at them.

The Old Woman

"STARS AND MOONBEAMS!" THE OLD WOMAN exclaimed. "And who might you young ladies be?" Her eyes were so sharp and gray, they sent a shiver down Tansy's spine.

But when the old woman stepped outside in her baggy flowered dress, suddenly she didn't seem so frightening anymore. After introducing herself and her friends, Tansy said, "We're searching for my two brothers. I wonder if you've seen them."

"They look a lot like her," Lysandra added helpfully. "Only they're bigger and hairier."

"One has dark hair and lots of muscles," said Fatima. "The other is sandy haired and a bit shorter."

"And they're on horseback," said Elena.

The old woman ran a bony hand through long, wispy hair. "Nay. I've not seen hide nor hair of them."

Tansy's shoulders slumped. "Oh."

"Be they lost, my child?" the old woman asked kindly.

"I don't know," said Tansy. "We've been searching, but we can't find them. They went hunting this morning, only we're not sure . . . that is, we think maybe . . ." Her voice trailed off. She was uncertain of whether to say more.

But the old woman didn't need to be told

what Tansy was thinking. "Stars and moonbeams!" she exclaimed again. "I suppose they be after the ogre!"

Sighing, Tansy nodded.

The old woman shook her head. "I tells them and I tells them," she muttered, "but I be just an old woman. And they be hotheaded young fools. They won't listen to me. More's the pity, says I."

"Excuse me, please," Elena said politely. "But who are 'they'? And *what* do you tell them?"

Fixing the princesses with her sharp, gray-eyed stare, the old woman pushed the cottage door open wider. "Come inside, dearies. I be just about to make tea, and then we can sit and have a chat."

Before they went inside, Lysandra picked up a piece of broken shingle from beside the door. Winking at Tansy, she pretended to bite into it. "Just making sure it's not made of gin-gerbread," she whispered.

Tansy stifled a giggle. The old woman might look like a witch, but she seemed kindly enough. Besides, whoever heard of a witch wearing a baggy flowered dress?

The cottage was only large enough for a tiny kitchen and a cozy living room. There was nowhere to sit except for a rocking chair in the middle of a woven rug. The princesses settled on the rug, politely leaving the chair for the old woman while she put a kettle on the stove to boil.

"Eight young men in eight years," the old woman said, joining the princesses. "All be turned to stone." She sighed. "Such a waste."

"Did they all stop here before they tried to fight the ogre?" Elena asked.

Rocking back and forth in her chair, the old woman nodded. "I tells them to go home.

I tells them the ogre means no harm. But not a one of 'em listens. They laughs at me. Then they rushes off." She tapped the side of her nose. "But I be knowing things they don't know."

"What kind of things?" asked Tansy.

The kettle whistled, and the old woman
started to rise. But Elena jumped up first.
"Please relax," she said. "I'll make the tea."

"I'll help," offered Lysandra. They found a
tin of tea in the cupboard and poured cups
for everyone.

"Thank you, dearie," said the old woman. She blew on her tea to cool it. "There be a way to face the ogre and not be turned to stone."

Tansy's eyes widened. "How?"

"By wearing a veil."

Fatima sipped her tea. "A veil?"

"Aye. To cover your eyes." The old woman gazed at Fatima's filmy purple pantaloons. "I be thinking the fabric in those be good for veils."

Fatima almost choked on her tea. "We'll keep that in mind," she replied. "Thanks."

As the princesses prepared to leave, Lysandra untangled her hair from the straps of the purse she always wore around her neck— a *magic* purse that never emptied of coins. She reached inside and then slipped a few gold pieces into the old woman's hand. "I hope you'll accept these coins in gratitude for your hospitality and advice."

The old woman's eyes misted over. "Thank you, dearie, and good luck!" she exclaimed as the princesses seated themselves on Fatima's flying carpet. "If you be seeing the ogre, don't be afraid. Look with your hearts, not with your eyes."

The princesses waved good-bye as they sailed away.

"One more thing," the old woman called to them. "Be using your gifts!"

"What do you suppose she meant by 'looking with our hearts' and 'using our gifts'?" Tansy asked as the flying carpet cleared the treetops.

"I'm not sure," said Elena.

Lysandra shuddered. "Let's hope we never need to know."

"Where to now?" Fatima asked.

Tansy thought for a moment. "Let's fly to the woods near the ogre's camp," she said. "We can watch for my brothers from there. If we can't stop them, at least we can give them the old woman's advice."

Fatima guided the carpet north again, until they could see the ogre's shack and the stone well.

Counting the statues, Tansy gasped. *"Ten!"* she cried. "We're too late!"

Statues

FATIMA LANDED THE FLYING CARPET NEAR THE well, and Tansy jumped off. She raced to the statues of her brothers. As if he'd been charging the ogre the instant he changed to stone, Edward's body stretched forward, his sword held high. There was a fierce scowl on his face. James, however, knelt on the ground, his hands flung up in horror.

"I should've stopped them," Tansy sobbed.

"It's all my fault. Poor Edward and James! How will I tell my family?"

Elena ran to Tansy and gave her a hug.

"Bats and bullfrogs!" muttered Fatima. "You didn't make your brothers go after the ogre. You weren't even sure that's what they were up to! And you *did* try to stop them."

Lysandra's forehead wrinkled with concern. "There's got to be a way to restore them to life."

"We could try my lotion." Elena pulled a small blue bottle out of her pocket.

Tansy stared at the bottle. She knew that Elena's lotion was magical. A small dab could make cuts and bruises disappear. But could it turn her brothers from stone to flesh?

"Wait a second," said Fatima. Reaching down, she ripped off the bottom halves of her pantaloons. "Veils," she said, dividing the filmy purple fabric into four long pieces. "Well, more like blindfolds, really. In case the ogre sees us."

"I certainly hope that old woman knew what she was talking about," Lysandra said as the princesses tied the fabric over their eyes.

The blindfolds made everything look fuzzy, but Tansy could see well enough to watch Elena pour out a small amount of lotion. Poor James, Tansy thought as Elena rubbed the lotion over his granite hands. He'd be so embarrassed if he knew they'd all seen him this way, kneeling and begging for his life. If the lotion worked, she wouldn't mention how scared he'd looked. "How long does it take?" Tansy asked when nothing happened right away.

Elena frowned. "It usually doesn't take

more than a few seconds."

Fatima and Lysandra stayed silent, but Tansy could see the pity in their eyes. Staring hard at James's hands, she willed him to come to life. But a few minutes passed, and still nothing happened.

"Maybe I just didn't use enough lotion." Elena dabbed a bit more onto James's hands.

At that exact moment, a tremendous roar split the air.

Tansy turned around, then froze in horror. So did the others. Still roaring, the ogre stood before them, spit flying from his

mouth. His features were blurred by their blindfolds, but the princesses could see that the ogre was hideously ugly. He had a huge, shaggy head with thick, slobbering lips, a sloping forehead, and extremely furry eyebrows. Covered with a coat of brown bushy hair, the ogre stood taller than a church steeple, and his legs were as big around as tree trunks.

The ogre roared again. Even though her knees were shaking, Tansy forced herself to stand up straight. "I don't suppose you speak English," she said.

The ogre responded by roaring right in Tansy's face. He seemed awfully angry, and his breath smelled horrible—worse than cooked cabbage and onion.

"I think that's a no," Lysandra whispered.

Suddenly the ogre stopped roaring.

Staring at the princesses, he scratched his head, looking confused.

"He's probably wondering why we haven't turned to stone," said Fatima. "I think these blindfolds are working."

"Hooray for that," said Lysandra. "Now he'll probably just *eat* us."

The ogre began to whimper.

"I wish I knew what he was trying to say," Elena whispered.

"My flute!" Tansy exclaimed, pulling it out of her pocket. She didn't know why she hadn't thought of it before. Maybe *that's* what the old woman had meant when she said they should use their gifts. Though her flute had worked its magic on humans many times, could it reveal the thoughts of an ogre in a language the princesses could understand? After all, Elena's gift—her magic lotion—hadn't helped. Still, anything was worth a try. Being careful to keep her blindfold in place, Tansy brought her flute to her lips and began to play.

The Ogre's Story

To the girls' surprise, the ogre fell silent. His eyes took on a dreamy look. Carried along by the melody, his thoughts drifted upward. *Pretty music*, he was thinking. *So soothing.* His hands—amazingly clean, with long, slender fingers—waved gently in time to the music.

But now the ogre's eyes darkened, and his thoughts shifted. *I only want to be left alone in peace. Why must humans plague me? Eight years ago, before I fled to this place, humans killed my husband and sons!*

Husband? thought Tansy. Well, what do you know? The ogre was female, then. An *ogress*, actually.

As Tansy continued to play, the door to the ogress's shack opened and a small ogre— not much taller than a full-grown human— stepped shyly outside. It had the same thick lips and sloping forehead as the ogress, but its cheeks were round and dimpled and it had lots of curly brown hair on top of its head. Its eyes widened when it saw the princesses.

Tansy was so surprised, she almost stopped playing her flute. *It's a child*, she thought.

The ogress must have understood Tansy, because she whirled around in alarm and roared a warning to her child: *Keep away!*

But drawn by the music, the small ogre limped downhill to its mother. Its left leg was wrapped in a bandage.

"Poor thing," murmured Elena.

The ogress hugged her child. *Oh, my sweet daughter. Just look how those bad men have wounded you!*

Tansy pulled her flute away from her mouth. Edward and James must have hurt the ogress's child! She felt so ashamed.

Pulling her small blue bottle from the pocket of her gown, Elena approached the ogress and child. Roaring, the ogress reared back.

"Quick," Tansy said, lifting her flute to her lips. "Let her know you mean no harm."

As Tansy played a soothing melody, Elena's thoughts soared above the music. *Please let me help your daughter. I have a lotion that may heal her wound.*

The ogress relaxed and allowed Elena to unwind the bandage from her daughter's leg. There was a nasty cut just below her knee. Tansy suspected it came from Edward's sword. *Don't be afraid, child,* Elena thought as she dabbed lotion over the wound. *This should make you feel better.*

The lotion's magic did its work and, within seconds, the wound had disappeared completely.

The ogress's daughter smiled. Jumping and skipping, she roared with happiness. *Look at me, Mother! My leg is healed. I'm well again!*

The ogress looked around at all four

princesses. *Thank you,* she thought. Then she pointed uphill to her shack. *I don't have much to offer, but would you please stay for lunch?*

The girls followed the ogress and her daughter into the shack. Its roof beams towered above the princesses, but the ogress could barely stand without hitting her head. A gigantic iron kettle hung in the fireplace, but to the princesses' relief, the ogress showed no intention of cooking and eating them.

In fact, lunch turned out to be vegetable soup and bread. Tansy put down her flute to eat. Afterward, the ogress showed them the huge garden behind her house. It was filled with carrots, potatoes, peas, and tomatoes— and all kinds of flowers.

Motioning to Tansy to play her flute again, the ogress asked, *Why do humans hate ogres?*

They're afraid of you, thought Lysandra.

They don't understand you, thought Fatima.

They think that you start fires and steal their sheep, thought Tansy. *And that maybe you'll eat them!*

The ogress's furry eyebrows drew together. *But I don't even eat meat!* she thought. *Can you tell them that?*

We can try, thought Elena.

The princesses smiled at one another. Tansy was sure they were all thinking the same thing: Not only was the ogre an *ogress,* but she was a vegetarian, too!

The ogress's daughter had been playing in the garden, digging in the dirt with a stick. Now she ran up to her mother and hugged her. The ogress glanced down at her daughter's leg, which showed no trace of its earlier wound. *You are the first humans to be kind to us,*

she thought. *I wish there was something I could do for you.*

Tansy's heart skipped a beat, but she kept on playing. *Perhaps there is something you could do,* she thought. *Those stone statues . . . could you make them human again?*

Back to the Castle

THROWING BACK HER SHAGGY HEAD, THE OGRESS roared so loudly, the princesses' ears rang. *How can you ask me that?* she thought. *Those men tried to kill my daughter!!*

I know. Tansy gulped. *But two of those men are my brothers.*

The ogress frowned. *Then I am sorry for you.*

Please give them a second chance, pleaded Tansy. *We can explain what we've learned about* you. *We can make sure no one ever bothers you again.*

The ogress's frown deepened. *I'd like to believe you, but how can I take the chance? You don't look much older than my daughter. Why would other humans listen to what you say?*

Tansy straightened her shoulders and nodded toward her friends. *Because we're princesses. My father is king of Majesta. He has never believed the rumors the villagers spread about you. If you free the men, the villagers will see you mean no harm. My father will give you his protection.*

The ogress cast a glance over her garden and home. *And my daughter and I can stay here as long as we want? No one will try to make us leave?*

Tansy nodded. *I promise.*

The ogress sighed heavily. *All right. Wait here.* She lumbered into the shack, returning a few minutes later with a small cloth pouch. She handed the pouch to Tansy. *There's powder inside. Throw a tiny pinch over each statue's head.*

Tansy's face lit up. *Thank you so much! I promise you won't regret this.* The ogress's hand was too large to shake, so she squeezed one of her fingers instead.

The ogress and her daughter waited inside their shack while Tansy and her friends raced down to the well. Tansy opened the pouch, drew out a pinch of the powder, and threw it over James's head. Flecked with gold and silver, the powder sparkled as it fell. Immediately the granite melted into warm, rosy flesh.

Still on his knees, James glanced up in confusion at Tansy and the other princesses. Then he leaped to his feet, his cheeks red with embarrassment. "I ... uh ... I was looking for something. A ... a ... *rock* to throw at the ogre," he stammered. "Hey—what are you doing here? And what are those funny purple things you're wearing over your eyes?"

"We'll explain in a minute," said Tansy. "But first we need to free the others." She opened the pouch wide so she and her friends could all take pinches of powder to toss over Edward and the rest of the statues.

Sneezing violently as the powder drifted over him, Edward waved his sword in the air. "Take that, you fire-setting, sheep-eating, spell-casting—"

"STOP!" shouted Tansy, quickly stepping back to avoid being sliced in two.

Edward stared at Tansy and her friends, looking just as bewildered as the other young men. Then they all began asking questions at once.

Tansy waved her arms in the air. "Be quiet and we'll explain."

The men sat on the ground before them, and the princesses took turns telling their story. They told about trying to follow Edward and James on Fatima's flying carpet. They described the old woman they'd met, and the good advice she'd given. Finally, they explained what Tansy's flute had revealed about the ogress and her daughter.

After the princesses finished speaking, the young men remained quiet for a long time. "I feel kind of foolish now," one of them said at last.

"Me too," said another.

Edward bowed his head. "I wounded a *child*," he said, sounding ashamed.

"But she's okay now," Elena reminded him softly.

James ran a hand through his hair. "You're saying the ogre is really an ogress and she's a *vegetarian?*"

Tansy nodded. "That's right."

"Well, I guess she wouldn't steal sheep then," he said.

"No," said Tansy. "And I'm sure she didn't do any of those other horrible things she's been accused of, either. She only wants to live in peace."

James scrambled to his feet. "Maybe we should go and apologize."

"That's a great idea," said Tansy. "Only you'll need to wear blindfolds. And I'll need mine to play my flute so the ogress can understand your thoughts."

It was decided that Edward, James, and a

young man named Steven would go to see the ogress. "Of course the blindfolds would have to be *purple*," Edward grumbled as they approached the shack. "That's a *girl* color."

Tansy smiled. "It's a *royal* color too, you know."

When the ogress opened the door, Tansy raised her flute and began to play. Many thoughts swirled through the air.

Thank you for releasing us, thought Steven.

I'm sorry I believed things about you that weren't true, thought James.

I'm sorry I hurt your daughter, thought Edward. *I'm glad she's okay now.*

The ogress was so pleased with their apologies that she gave them vegetables from her garden to share with their families and the other young men.

By now it was late afternoon. Edward's and

James's horses had disappeared after their masters had changed into statues. James frowned. "I guess we'll have to walk back to the castle."

Fatima eyed the brothers. "It'll be a squeeze," she said, "but I think I can fit two more on my carpet."

When all six of them were seated as comfortably as possible, they waved good-bye to the eight young men returning home on foot. With the added weight of Edward and James, the carpet rose more slowly than usual, but soon it had cleared the treetops and was soaring toward the castle.

"Wow! You can see everything from up here!" James exclaimed.

Edward said nothing. As they picked up speed, his face turned as white as the snow on Mount Majesta, and his knuckles gripped the edge of the carpet. Suddenly Tansy realized why Edward always refused to climb the stairs to her tower room. She hid a smile. Her biggest, strongest, oldest brother—who'd shown no fear in facing what he thought was a ferocious ogre—was afraid of heights!

Trouble

It was nearly dusk by the time Fatima landed the carpet near the castle. Tansy's two younger brothers were playing outside, lunging at each other with toy swords. They came running toward Tansy as she climbed off the carpet.

Cole planted himself in front of his sister. "You're really in big trouble," he said. "You didn't tell Mother and Father where you were going!"

"Yeah," echoed Ethan. "You just disappeared."

It was true, Tansy admitted. But how could she have known what would happen? She'd thought they would find Edward and James right away.

Color was returning to Edward's face now that they had landed. "Clear off, you two," he growled at Cole and Ethan.

Laughing, the two boys ran off.

Fatima rolled up her carpet and strapped it onto her back. As everyone headed toward the castle, James whispered to Tansy, "Maybe Father will forgive us when he finds out what we've learned about the ogre—I mean, the *ogress*."

Tansy hoped so. But she didn't think King Albert would be pleased that his two oldest sons had disobeyed his orders. What if the ogress *hadn't* had a magical powder to restore James and Edward to life?

Queen Charlotte met them just inside the
Main Hall. For once she was not her usual
cheerful self. Wrapping Edward, James, and
Tansy in a big hug, she sobbed. "Thank good-

ness you're home. We were so worried about you! How did you manage to escape from the horrible ogre?"

Tansy frowned. *Escape?* It was true Edward

and James had been turned into statues, but the ogress had helped to free them in the end. She'd been nothing but kind to the princesses.

Edward stroked his straggly beard. "How did you know where we'd gone?"

"We didn't, for sure," said Queen Charlotte. "But when your horses came back without you, and we couldn't find the girls, we talked to Jonah. He told us the princesses had asked him where you'd gone and had flown off soon afterward. He guessed they'd left to search for you, thinking you'd gone to find the ogre."

The queen gazed at Tansy and her friends tearfully. "We feared the ogre had captured and eaten you all. Ogres like princesses, I've been told. They think royal girls taste sweet."

Fatima made a face. "Why should princesses taste *sweet*? I'm sure *I'd* taste as nasty as skunk cabbage!"

Popping up from behind the large potted fern, Cole grinned. "Tansy would probably taste like a smelly old *shoe*!"

Tansy rolled her eyes. "Who cares what we'd taste like!" She quickly explained all that had happened that day and what they'd learned about the ogress.

Queen Charlotte listened carefully. Her eyes widened when Tansy mentioned finding Edward and James as statues. When Tansy finished, the queen cried, "But this is *terrible!*"

"*What's* terrible?" asked Tansy. "Don't you see? The ogress didn't do any of those horrible things she was accused of. She only wants to live with us in peace."

"No," said her mother, shaking her head. "You don't understand. What's terrible is that your father rode off with Jonah and Matthew and about a dozen village men a few hours ago. Your father didn't want to believe the rumors, but when Edward's and James's horses came back without them . . ." She sighed. "They're planning to sneak up on the ogre tonight while he—I mean, *she*—is asleep . . . and set fire to her shack!"

Tansy felt as if she'd just been punched in the stomach. "Oh no!" she moaned.

"We've got to save her!" cried Lysandra.

Elena nodded in agreement.

"We'll fly back on my carpet," said Fatima. "With any luck, we'll be able to reach the men before they reach the ogress's house."

"Yes," said Tansy. She didn't want to think about what might happen if they *weren't* lucky.

"I'm coming too," declared James.

"So am I," said Edward, turning white as

he eyed the magic carpet.

Before they left, Tansy asked her mother for a bolt of gauzy white fabric the queen had been saving to make curtains. "What do you want it for?" Queen Charlotte asked as she handed it to Tansy.

"I'll explain later," Tansy said hurriedly.

"Be careful, and come home safely!" the queen called to them as they ran outside. The princesses, along with Edward and James, climbed onto the carpet and rose into the sky.

Night had fallen, but the moon was almost full, casting a glow that lit their way. Clutching the bolt of fabric, Tansy anxiously scanned the forest and meadows below for signs of horses and men. But she couldn't see any torches gleaming among the trees, and she couldn't hear voices, or hooves beating the ground.

"Where could they be?" Elena finally asked, voicing the question on all of their minds.

When at last they reached the well, there was still no sign of the men or their horses. The ogress's shack stood a short distance away, seemingly untouched. Tansy sighed with relief. Perhaps her father and the villagers had decided not to harm the ogress after all. Seeing the statues gone, they might have realized the young men had been set free. Or perhaps they'd even met up with a few of them returning home and learned the story of their release. If so, King Albert and his men might be headed back to the castle this very minute.

"I guess they're not here," said Lysandra. "Do you think we should wait, just in case we missed them somehow?"

Everyone started talking at once. Suddenly Edward held a finger to his lips. "Shh," he whispered. "I think I hear something."

They all grew quiet. For a minute the only sounds were the wind in the trees and the flapping of bats' wings. But then Tansy heard something else—the soft whinny of a horse. Glancing at the others, she knew they'd heard it too. All at once bright orange flames shot up from the roof of the shack, and a group of riders—bursting from behind the ogress's home—galloped away.

Fire!

Horrified, Tansy watched as flames spread from the roof of the shack down the sides. "Halt!" shouted Edward as the riders thundered up to the well. They stopped abruptly, their horses rearing up in confusion.

"Edward?" King Albert's eyes darted from him to James to the princesses. "We thought the ogre had killed you all! What happened?

How did you escape?"

Tansy tugged at Edward's sleeve. "If we don't act fast, the ogress and her daughter will be burned alive!"

"You're right!" Edward exclaimed. "We've got to save them and put out the fire!"

King Albert frowned. *"Ogress? Daughter?"*

"Ask James," Tansy said. Tearing two strips from the bolt of gauzy fabric, she threw one to Edward, then tied the other around her own eyes. "Here," she said, tossing the bolt to Elena.

With Jonah's help, Elena made sure everyone had a blindfold so they could face the ogress without turning to stone. After they were all fitted, they formed a line behind Fatima. She was already at the well, hauling up buckets of water to throw on the fire.

Meanwhile, Tansy and Edward raced

toward the burning shack. As Edward forced open the door, Tansy pulled out her flute and began to play. Flames licked the wooden house. Tansy wiped sweat from her forehead. When the door was finally open, smoke rolled out and Edward disappeared inside. Tansy heard a loud roar as the ogress awoke.

Don't be alarmed, Edward thought. *We're here to help you.*

I smell smoke, thought the ogress.

It's a fire! thought Edward. *You must get out quickly!*

Seconds later the ogress and her daughter crawled from the shack, coughing. They were

followed by Edward. He sprawled on the ground, gasping for breath.

Tansy bent over him. "Are you okay?" she asked anxiously.

To her surprise, he reached up and hugged her. "You're a wonder with that flute," he said. "Who would've thought we'd make such a good team?"

Tansy smiled and hugged him back.

By now buckets of water were being passed hand over hand down the long line that stretched from the well to the shack. Lysandra and Matthew were nearest to the fire, working together to heave water at the flames.

Slowly the ogress stood, her fearsome figure towering over everyone. Some of the men gasped, and Tansy remembered how frightened she'd felt the first time she saw her. But when the ogress hugged her daughter tight—tears streaming down her face—the men relaxed. Perhaps they could see she was only a mother, and when it came right down to it, not so very different from their own.

Finally, after much work, the raging fire was quenched. Roaring sadly, the ogress and her daughter stared at the charred remains of their home. King Albert motioned for Tansy to play her flute so the ogress could hear his thoughts. As Tansy played, her father faced the ogress, but his thoughts drifted out to everyone. *I am so sorry. We were afraid of you, and we let our fear get the best of us.*

Still holding her daughter, the ogress rocked back and forth, moaning. *Not all ogres are monsters,* she thought. *We only want to live in peace.*

King Albert hung his head. *That's what we*

want too. If you'll let us, we'll help rebuild your home. We'll be your friends.

At this, the ogress's thick lips stretched upward into what could only be a smile.

Edward, James, and some of the other men volunteered to stay behind to rebuild the ogress's shack. Meanwhile, King Albert, the rest of the men, and the princesses prepared for home.

"Can Jonah and I ride on your flying carpet?" Matthew asked Fatima shyly.

"Sure," Fatima replied. "But what about your horses?"

"I don't think they'd fit," Jonah joked. "But they can follow Father back to the castle."

When everyone was seated, the carpet lifted high into the air. As they glided away from the mountain, Jonah looked back and gave a whoop. "Now *this* is the way to travel! I'm going to have to paint a picture of how

Mount Majesta looks from the sky!"

Tansy smiled. Having brothers wasn't so bad, she decided. Of course, they didn't always behave the way you wanted them to. But sometimes, like Edward, they could pleasantly surprise you.

Good News

Pounding, thumping, and shouting woke Tansy the next morning. "Is that you, Jonah?" she called out before realizing the noises weren't coming from outside her door after all. They were coming from somewhere else in the castle.

The other princesses had been awakened by the noise as well. They all climbed out of bed, shivering in the cold morning air, and pulled warm robes over their nightgowns. They donned slippers, then trooped downstairs to find out what was happening.

An older man carrying a ladder strode past them at the bottom of the stairs, followed by a younger man pushing a cartful of rocks. "Morning, princesses!" the younger man called out cheerfully.

"Morning," the princesses replied.

"Hey, he was one of the statues," Fatima declared after the men had disappeared from view.

Of course! Tansy had thought he looked familiar.

Queen Charlotte was sitting in front of a roaring fire, sipping a cup of tea and reading, when the girls entered the Main Hall. She looked up from her book. "Good morning," she said, sounding even more cheerful than ever. "I bet you're hungry for breakfast."

As her friends warmed their hands in front of the fire, Tansy glanced into the Dining Room. The table was covered with an amazing array of fruits, breads, eggs, and meats.

Elena appeared beside Tansy. "Just look at that food!" she exclaimed. "Where do you suppose it all came from?"

Before they could ask Queen Charlotte, King Albert stepped into the hall. He beamed at the princesses and gave Tansy a big hug. "I've just sent out a message with the good news about our *gentle* ogress. Already word of the young men's release has spread. People are returning to the kingdom!"

Tansy clapped her hands together. "That's great!" Her friends nodded in agreement.

Three men clattered into the Main Hall, passing through with hammers, chisels, and buckets. "What's going on?" Lysandra asked.

"Isn't it wonderful?" Queen Charlotte

said. "The young men you helped to release have come with their families to repair the castle. And they've even brought platters of delicious food."

"Fantastic!" said Tansy. The sorry state of her family's castle hadn't made a bit of difference to her friends, but it would be nice to live in a place that was less drafty and crumbling. And perhaps they'd even have servants again, since people were returning to the kingdom.

Jonah came into the hall, carrying a newly painted picture. "It's about time you were up!" he exclaimed to the girls. Then he showed them his picture—a grand view of Mount Majesta.

"Is that us?" asked Elena, pointing to a tiny flying carpet in the corner.

Squinting, Tansy could just make out six small figures on top of the carpet.

Jonah smiled. "That's right."

The princesses helped themselves to the pastries and fruit. Jonah had eaten earlier, but he stayed around for a second breakfast. "I'd sure like to fly on your carpet again," he said to Fatima. "I'd like to try to paint an aerial view this time."

"If Jonah goes, may I come too?" asked

Matthew.

"I'd be glad to take you both," said Fatima.

"Why don't we all go?" Tansy suggested. "We could fly to the ogress's camp, check up on Edward and James, and see how the work is going."

"Great idea," said Lysandra. "Let's do it!"

After breakfast the princesses got dressed while Jonah and Matthew cleared the table and washed the dishes. Then they all gathered outside.

Fatima unrolled her carpet. "All aboard!" she called out. Quickly the friends scrambled to take their places.

As they sailed into the sky above a sea of leafy green, Jonah leaned toward Elena. "Isn't the view incredible? Mount Majesta looks beautiful from above the trees!"

Elena nodded. "I bet you're getting ideas for more paintings."

"Don't encourage him," Matthew grumbled. "He's already painted Mount Majesta from every angle and in every kind of weather and season."

Jonah sighed dramatically. "True art is often underappreciated and misunderstood."

"You could say that about a lot of things,"

Tansy said slyly. "*Sisters*, for example."

"Or ogres," said Elena.

Tansy lifted her face to the sun and took a breath of fresh air. She felt happy that everything had turned out so well and that, once again, she and her friends had chanced upon a marvelous adventure.

Check out all of the Princess Power adventures!

Princess Power #1:
The Perfectly Proper Prince

Princess Lysandra finds sewing, napping, and decorating the palace to be extremely boring. She wants adventure! So when Lysandra meets Fatima, Elena, and Tansy, she couldn't be happier. But their first quest comes even sooner than expected, when they stumble upon a frog that just *might* have royal blood running through his veins.

Princess Power #2:
The Charmingly Clever Cousin

Princess Fatima doesn't care much for her brother-in-law, Ahmed. His cousin Yusuf is much more charming, with his elegant mustache and impressive magic tricks. Yet when Ahmed goes to visit his dying father—and never returns—Fatima starts to worry. Something suspicious is going on, and it just might be up to the princesses to come to the rescue!

Princess Power #3:
The Awfully Angry Ogre

Princess Tansy knows that whenever something terrible occurs in her kingdom, the ogre gets the blame. Yet anyone who challenges him is turned to stone! Tansy's two oldest brothers have been forbidden to fight the ogre, but they're determined to try. Can Tansy and her friends save the boys from a horrible fate?

Princess Power #4:
The Mysterious, Mournful Maiden

Princess Elena is excited to find a treasure on the beach—a beautiful comb that tames and softens her frizzy hair. However, she soon starts dreaming of a green-haired maiden who cries that she can't live without her comb. The princesses all want to help. But will they be able to find the maiden . . . before it's too late?

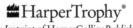

HarperTrophy®
An Imprint of HarperCollins*Publishers*

www.harpercollinschildrens.com